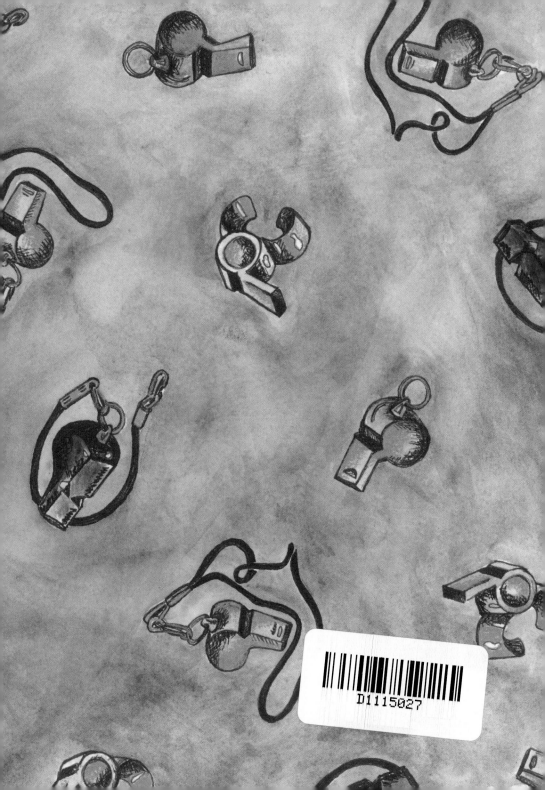

Praise for *The Official Adventures Series* and *Drop the Puck: Hockey Every Day, Every Way*

"I love the way this book celebrates individual differences, strengths, and similarities. When children learn about themselves, others, and the world around them, that is the ultimate hat trick."
—Aimee Jordan, Lila's mom and fierce advocate for people with disabilities

"It's really cool to see my name as a character in a book, especially a children's book. I hope it helps other kids to be inspired to think, create, and invent. It's neat to think my name might motivate readers to get out there and do things and DREAM BIG like I did because I know what it's like to be one of them."
—Tripp Phillips, president and inventor, Le-Glue

"I grew up as the typical Minnesota kid. Hockey is my life. These books are a hat trick!"
—Luke Delzer, inspiration for the character "Luke," Totino-Grace High School Varsity

Praise for *The Official Adventures Series* and *Drop the Puck, Let's Play Hockey!*

"Minnesota kids love hockey and this story teaches young people about respect, sportsmanship and to play with a great attitude! We are cheering for the Minnesota Bears and Breezer!"
—Senator Karin and Phil Housley, Assist. Coach, Nashville Predators

"This book series teaches children about respecting each other and reaching for your dreams! We have a dorm room and UND green jersey waiting for Avery!"
—Hon. Mark Kennedy, President, University of North Dakota

"The Official Adventures Series books are terrific heart-warming stories that celebrate hockey, family and children with special needs! Our family loves these hockey tales that teach life lessons and encourages everyone to treat others with respect."
—Bridget and Matt Cullen, Two-Time Stanley Cup Champion

"A fun story with a valuable message. What we love most is that every child feels like a STAR! Go Minnesota Bears!"
—Kary and Matt Carkner, NHL Veteran, Assist. Coach, Bridgeport Sound

ISBN 13: 978-1-63489-043-4
LCCN: 2016952987
Printed in the United States of America
First Printing: 2016

23 22 21 20   5 4 3 2

Book design and typesetting by Tiffany Daniels.

Wise Ink Creative Publishing
807 Broadway St. NE, Suite #46
Minneapolis, MN 55413
wiseink.com

To order, visit www.itascabooks.com or call 1-800-901-3480.
Reseller discounts available.

Drop the Puck Let's Play Hockey

THE OFFICIAL ADVENTURES

BOOK 3

THE OFFICIAL ADVENTURES

Written by Jayne J. Jones Beehler

Illustrated by Katrina G. Dohm

To cozy homes where we hang our skates

A Note from Jayne and Katrina

The Official Adventures of brothers Blaine and Cullen continue with this third tale. Blaine and his new friend, Ann, were born with Down syndrome and have special needs. Down syndrome is a genetic disorder that can cause physical growth delays, characteristic facial features, and mild to moderate intellectual disability. Blaine and Ann's speech at times can be stuttering, slurring, and repetitive. It's time to Drop the Puck, Let's Play Hockey!

The Official Adventures Book Series:

And the story goes...
for the love of the game.

CHAPTER 1

A State Championship Victory without a Celly is like Peanut Butter without Jelly

With one eye half-open, Cullen rolled over, slapping the snooze button on his hockey alarm clock.

"Ohhh nnooo you don'ttt," snorted Blaine, who was already dressed and ready for their big day. From head to toe, Blaine wore his Hockeytown USA gear. His State Pee Wee Championship medal hung around his neck. He leaped and did a belly flop, landing smack on top of Cullen. The boys both moaned and burst into giggles.

"Get up! Youuuu need to ggeeet ready," Blaine urged, motioning for Cullen to get up.

"Slow your roll! Hockeytown USA's victory parade and celebration starts at 3:00 pm, not 3:00 am!" Cullen teased with a smile.

"Butttt, we caaann't be late!" shot back Blaine.

"Us, late? Not a chance. First to arrive, last one to leave. Just like the locker room." Cullen smirked.

"Yyyyess! Along with Avery and Paisley," added Blaine.

"Just a week ago, we were playing our hearts out. Today, we're celebrating our hearts out!" Avery announced to her teammates. They were gathered in front of three Hockeytown USA fire trucks.

"Avery, I gettt ssshotgun," Blaine announced awkwardly.

"Shotgun?" asked Luke. The teammates looked confused.

"Blaine, we ride on top of the truck, as a team. Waving to our fans!" Paisley said.

Blaine began nervously pacing back and forth. He looked up, trying to guess the height of the fire trucks. "IIIII think it's fffivvee feett above my armpits. I'mmm out," he broadcasted.

"You can climb the ladder with Aves and me. You can stand right between us," Luke said.

"It will be fun and safe," Avery said. "A team that plays together celebrates together!"

"I dddonn't know," Blaine replied. "It's high uppppp. Talllerrr than Ref Rylleee cann reach!"

"You can do it, bro. Make Ref Rylee proud," Cullen encouraged.

The streets of Hockeytown USA began to fill with parents, family and friends holding homemade signs. Many of the small town fans were excited for the post parade banquet. A special guest was coming to Hockeytown USA!

CHAPTER 2

Small Town Magic

The sirens of Hockeytown USA's police cars kicked off the parade. The high school marching band played traditional hockey fight songs. The fire trucks drove through town carrying the team as they waved to their families and fans!

It was a day and night like no other in Hockeytown USA, where hockey banquet traditions abound. Families brought their potluck hotdishes and bars. It was a homemade meal for champions.

"This tater-tot hotdish is incredible," Luke mumbled, smacking his lips."

"Now, this is what I call a P-A-R-T-Y!" said Avery as she ate and studied the crowd.

Blaine pointed. "I tthhiink I see my favorite tteacherr, Misssssss Marvin."

"She's cool," Paisley said. She looked around. "I think I see at least a hundred teachers in this crowd. This is awesome. Our little team is bringing everyone together."

"Hockey brings communities together. Small town magic," their coach said.

The lights dimmed. The table chatter ended. A spotlight lit the stage. "Thiissss is real coooll," Blaine snorted. Everyone laughed and hushed him.

A loudspeaker announced, "Ladies and gentlemen, hockey fans, welcome to the stage our emcees, America's favorite referees, Ref Rylee and Ref Rosee!"

The crowd clapped and jumped to their feet. Blaine fell back in shock. He accidentally pushed his chair too hard, flipping it over and falling onto the floor. Avery and Paisley quietly helped him recover.

"Good evening, Hockeytown USA! Congratulations to Minnesota's State Pee Wee champions!" Ref Rylee said. "We're thrilled to be here in the hometown of our friend, Blaine Ashton."

Blaine, blushing, sat in silence, his mouth open in awe.

Ref Rylee continued, "Tonight, we are celebrating a tremendous team, a courageous win, and a favored hockey community. With us we have one of America's hockey greats, live in-person in Hockeytown USA. We also have a special video from Matthew "Ace" Acerllo. And last but not least, the Pee Wee champs will each share their tourney memories!" Ref Rosee directed.

CHAPTER 3

Microphones, Memories, and Dreams

Luke turned to his table of teammates. "What did Ref Rylee say?" he asked. He hadn't known each player would have to speak on stage to the large crowd. The thought made him choke on his orange drink. His dad winked reassuringly.

"Shut the rink door," Avery blasted. "I can't wait! Hand me the microphone now! Move over, Erin Andrews!"

Suddenly the arena went quiet. A video of Ace began to play on a large screen above the stage. "Every day is a great day for hockey in Hockeytown USA! Congrats to the Pee Wees! In the game we all love, and in life, you always give it your all and do your best. You hustle, you dangle, you score, and you set goals, some of which you score and some you miss." Ace pointed at the camera. "But whatever you do, never quit."

The video ended, and Ref Rosee stepped forward. "Hockey fans, please welcome to Hockeytown USA America's hockey great, Jeremy 'JR' Roenick!"

Everyone in the arena rose to their feet. JR came onto the stage and immediately went into the crowd. He shook hands with each of the Pee Wee players. When he got to Blaine, he leaned over and whispered, "Could you come on stage with me?"

Blaine looked at Cullen, his eyes wide with panic. Avery gave Blaine a hard push, nudging him out of his seat. He turned to JR and nodded nervously.

JR smiled as he led Blaine to the stage. When they reached the podium, he faced the audience. "Thank you, State of Hockey and Hockeytown USA!" he said. "There are no better hockey fans . . . except in Chicago!" The crowd roared with laughter, and a few good-humored boos. "I love Hockeytown USA!" he continued. "I especially love the heart of your state-crowned champion Pee Wee team. To them, it's more than a game. They understand the importance of everyone's job on the team, and that every player, has talents and abilities. This is why I have exciting news: I've talked with a few of my friends. Together, we're proud to announce the American Special Hockey Association is coming to Hockeytown USA!" JR wrapped his arm around Blaine. "I've got your new jersey right here, buddy." He pulled a bright purple jersey from inside the podium! "Number Twenty-Seven is ready for ice again!"

Everyone rose to their feet. Blaine looked for his parents in the cheering crowd. He saw his parents and grandparents cheering!

Avery, Paisley, Luke, and Cullen were fist bumping each other.

Ref Rylee joined JR and Blaine on stage. "Wow, America's favorite hockey manager lacing up skates! We can't wait to come watch, Blaine! And you get the infamous Number Twenty-Seven! Watch out, JR, Blaine's coming after your records!"

"I hope he crushes them all," JR joked.

"I, I, I, I won't letttt you down. I will hhuustle," Blaine replied.

JR smiled. "We have no doubt."

Ref Rylee stepped forward to address the audience. "Friends, we just heard from Blaine. Now it's time to hear from the rest of the state champion's squad." He motioned toward the young team. All of them nervously piled onto the stage.

For a moment none of them approached the microphone. Then

Paisley, who wasn't one of the nervous nellies, stepped up. "I want to thank my family for coming to every game. Driving me to practice. It means the world to me. Stay tuned for later—Avery and I have major breaking news to share at the end of this celly!" She quickly passed the microphone to Cullen, ignoring the questioning look Avery gave her.

"Thanks to all our fans," Cullen said. "I want to get back on the ice ASAP. This summer, Luke and I will be spending a month at Minnesota Hockey Camps. Avery better watch out—my speed and stride will be hard to beat after four weeks in Nisswa with Minnesota's best!" His teammates all laughed as he passed the microphone to Luke.

Luke's eyes were fixed on his shoes. "Thank you. Aw, um, um, rad thanks to my dad for being a great coach," he said, the words coming out in a mumbled rush. "It's usually not easy being the coach's kid, but this team makes it easy. Go Hockeytown USA."

Avery was last to get the microphone. She motioned for Paisley to join her. "I want to thank my parents. And, definitely my teammates. We love playing on the boy's team, even though our backs hurt … mainly from carrying your weight, Cullen." She looked over at him and winked.

Paisley, bursting with her news, pushed Avery aside. "Ladies and gentlemen, we need to wrap this party up before midnight so Avery and I can get to bed. We have an appointment to get our passports tomorrow because . . . we've been invited to a U10 international hockey festival in Finland this summer. We'll be temporarily trading our green jerseys, for red, white, and blue!"

The crowd rose again. Cheers of "USA! USA! USA!" filled the arena.

CHAPTER 4

Following Your Heart Always Leads to the Rink

"Did you check your email?" Luke asked.

"Yup! I printed the hockey camp packing list. Then I handed it off to Blaine to get started packing," Cullen said, grinning.

"Yoouuu ppaacck yourself!" Blaine replied. "I'm gggoing to misss you bottth!"

"Don't worry, hockey camp will go by fast," Cullen said. "Plus, you'll be playing every week too, Number Twenty-Seven!"

"And, your favorite neighborhood pet, Stanley Cup, will need twice-a-day walks," Luke added.

"Ittt wwonn'ttt bee the same," Blaine murmured.

Paisley grabbed her cell phone and texted Avery: *Poimi Unis huomenna. Tytöt jääkiekon sääntöjä!*

When Avery got the text, she laughed before replying, What? Tape too many hockey sticks today? LOL! Then she pasted the text into the Finnish-to-English app on her phone. "Pick up unis tomorrow. Girls hockey rules!" After some fast Internet searching, she found the perfect response: *Tytöt sääntö. Pojat kuolata myös Suomessa.* She couldn't hit send fast enough.

Paisley translated. "Girls rule. Boys drool, even in Finland!" She belly laughed and texted back *Kyllä*!

Avery didn't need to translate. She already knew *Kyllä* meant yes.

It was the last day of school before summer vacation. Blaine gave a good-bye hug to Miss Marvin and shared fist bumps with his school friends. As he strolled out the school door, he began to worry. His brother, Luke, Paisley, and Avery would soon leave for their hockey adventures. What would that mean for his plans for summer fun? Little did Blaine realize, but his very own summer hockey adventure was about to begin!

As he slowly wandered the aisles of the Bauer Hockey Store, Cullen's arms overflowed with hockey gear. Every cool item grabbed his attention as he thought about what he'd need for hockey camp.

His dad trailed behind him, hiding a smile. "I sure hope you have birthday money for all that," he said.

Before Cullen could answer, he spotted his mom and a Bauer sales associate helping Blaine measure his skate size. He went over to join them. "Hey, what's going on?" he said.

Blaine looked up. "I'm ggeetting ssskates," he said.

"That's awesome!" Cullen said. "Here's a mouth guard. You'll need it to nix all your talking!"

Blaine gasped and looked at his mom, who patted him on the shoulder. "Don't worry, honey, Cullen's just joking. Of course the ASHA coaches will let you talk!"

"Yeah, you'll be fine. Just focus on keeping your chin up and knees bent," Cullen said. "Besides, I have a feeling that pair of skates is lucky."

Blaine looked down at his skates, which the sales associate had finished lacing up. He tried to rise to his feet. After a few wobbles, he was able to stand straight. Blaine beamed with pride. He stepped forward with his right foot while the salesman put his thumb on the front edge of Blaine's left skate.

"Can you wiggle your big toe for me?" the salesman asked.

Blaine smiled while he wiggled his toe.

"By golly, I think these are a winner!" the salesman confirmed. "Just like you."

"Tttthaaank you!" Blaine said. He tried

to jump for joy but instead went headfirst over the store bench, doing a half-somersault.

Cullen guffawed "Sir, we'll also take a case of shin pads and helmets for this rookie!"

Later that night at home, Cullen peaked in on Blaine before going to bed. Blaine was already tucked in, his new skates on the nightstand.

Cullen tiptoed in and sat on the edge of his brother's bed. Blaine felt his presence but pretended to be asleep.

"I'm going to miss you, Blaine," Cullen whispered. "I can't wait to see you skate. Wait until I come home before you score your first goal. I want to be there to see it.

Love you, bro." He snuck out of the room and closed the door gently behind him.

Blaine stirred and rolled over, smiling to himself. He'd heard every word Cullen said.

CHAPTER 5

The Minnesota Bears

"Wow! Check out that line of skaters waiting to get on the ice!" said Blaine's mom.

Blaine looked over to where she was pointing but didn't say anything. "I-I-I'm nerrrvous," he finally whispered.

"Don't worry, champ," his dad said, opening the arena's mezzanine's door.

"Soon you'll have a whole team of best friends."

Each of his parents grabbed one of his new skates and helped Blaine lace up. His dad grabbed his helmet and positioned it perfectly on his son's head.

His mom stepped back to take a quick picture with her phone. "Cullen would be so proud!" she said, wiping away a tear. "I'm going to send this to him right now."

"Geettt a viddeeoo of me sskkatting tooo," Blaine said.

"Of course, we will," his dad said.

Blaine grabbed his dad's hand. Together they walked out of the mezzanine area and into the main ice arena. The ice was filled with young skaters, all anxious for their first Saturday practice of the summer season. Motionless, Blaine stood observing from the rink door.

Ref Rylee, an ASHA volunteer coach, noticed Blaine. He motioned to the Minnesota Bear's mascot, Breezer the Bear, who was on skates helping other beginners, to join him. Together, Breezer and Ref Rylee skated to Blaine.

"Hi Blaine!" Ref Rylee high-fived Blaine, knocking him off balance a bit. "Meet Breezer—he's a great ice skating partner!"

Blaine beamed. "I—I-I-I-I loovvvee massccots! And minnii donnutsss," he replied.

Breezer playfully shook Blaine's helmet and reached for his arm. Blaine looked at his parents, who both gave him a thumbs up. Blaine took a baby step forward onto the ice, then froze.

"Nice job!" Ref Rylee said. "Bend your knees a little more, then lift your feet like you're marching. Like this."

Blaine watched Ref Rylee closely and

tried to mirror his movements. He bent his knees a little too much and fell to the ice. Breezer, pretending to giggle, fell down next to Blaine. Ref Rylee did the same.

"Here's how to get back up!" Ref Rylee said. "Go on all fours, like a bear! Put one knee up and push up using your arm muscles on that knee."

As he talked, Breezer continued to fall down over and over, making Blaine giggle. After a few more attempts, Blaine finally stood and took a few strides forward. He looked into the bleachers. He spotted his parents, who were both holding up their phones to videotape him.

A young girl skated over to Blaine and Ref Rylee. She pretended to body check the coach before turning to Blaine. "Whaaat's yourrrr nnname?" she asked.

"B-b-b-lainee," he mumbled around his mouth guard.

She cocked her head. "DDDDDane? Likkke aaaaa great dddane?" she asked.

"No, just Blaine," Ref Rylee corrected. "He's new to the Bears. Blaine, this is Ann."

Ann grinned widely. "I llllike great ddddane betttter, so I thiinkkk Greattt Blainnne is gooddd!" she said. Blaine and Ref Rylee laughed. Ann grabbed Blaine's arm and Ref Rylee followed suit. Blaine's parents put down their phones and watched as the pair pulled Blaine around the ice, picking up speed as they went. After a few laps, they both let go of Blaine's arms. Just like hockey magic, Blaine was suddenly skating on his own.

As the practice continued, Blaine's parents watched in awe. Then a woman's voice said, "I remember Ann's first practice. Hard to believe she's been playing for ASHA for four years now!" Blaine's parents turned to see a smiling proud woman

standing near them. "I'm her mom," she
said, "and this is my husband."

"Nice to meet you," Blaine's dad said.
"She's a great skater—so fast, and what a
stride!"

Ann's dad grinned. "Yes, she's worked hard to get that good. Years in the making! ASHA really understands how to teach kids with special needs. All the coaches are patient, and they really make physical activity fun. They know it's about more than just learning hockey, it's about friendship."

"We love our Saturday mornings!" Ann's mom shared. "Ann gets to play her favorite game with her friends. The many benefits of special hockey are far reaching and amazing!"

Ann's parents sat down, and together the four of them watched the skaters. Blaine and Ann didn't leave each other's side until Ref Rylee ended the practice.

Later on, in the waiting room, Blaine's feet hurt, but he didn't tell anyone. "Ddaaaadd, I ddidid it!" he hooted as he kicked off his skates.

His mom smiled. "I know, we got you skating on video for Cullen."

Ann sat next to Blaine, and he turned to face her. "Youuuu wannnt to geetttt minni donnuts?" he asked.

"Mmmmmini ddddonuts, Greattt Blainnne? I-I-I like sushi!" Ann said, tossing her helmet in the air.

Blaine's dad gave them a quizzical look. "Great Blaine?"

"Itt'ssss mmyyyy nickname," Blaine answered quickly.

"Alllll ppllayers have nnnnicknames," Ann added.

"Oh really?" Blaine's mom asked. "What's yours?"

Ann snickered. "Ann!" she said. Everyone giggled.

CHAPTER 6

The Hockey Bag Smell

"**H**oly hockey breezers, Cabin Aspen!" said Lukey. "What in the world is that smell?" continued Luke while snooping around their cabin at Minnesota Hockey Camps. The cabins were painted in the team colors of the San Jose Sharks. Each cabin had a main living room area and bedrooms for campers to share. The historic hockey camp was decorated with first class hockey artifacts throughout. An antique giant bell is rung to begin and end camp each week.

Cullen took a big whiff. "Smells like hockey—fresh hockey!"

"Hockey mixed with mosquito spray and fish bait," Jagger Stephen, another young camper yelled.

Cullen sighed. "I love this place. I even love that smell. No place like hockey camp, in Nisswa, Minnesota. From the rink to the lake, from the lake to the rink!"

Every Saturday, the campers played in an end-of-camp hockey tourney. Parents of campers who were only there for the week came to watch the games and bring their campers home. Since Lukey and Cullen were month-long campers, their cabin formed Team Cabin Aspen and played every Saturday.

"It's been a fast two weeks. It seems like we just got here and ate our first Sunday night Grillo burger!" Luke said. Then his face brightened. "But we still have two more weeks to go! And, more flavors of Chocolate Ox ice cream to try."

"Definitely! Where every aisle is the candy aisle," McLaren, another camper chimed in. "Two more weeks of great ice, great drills, great teammates!" Jagger Stephen cheered. "And, don't forget great food!" Luke added.

Cullen pretended to skate across the room and take a slap shot. "I'm going to work on my wrist shot and puck handling this week. Next week, I'm going all five hole deep and conquering shooting!" He turned to Luke, Jagger Stephen and McLaren. "Can you guys believe we're 6-0 in tourney play? That's a camp record! I think we can take it all the way."

"We should tell Coach Grillo that if we go undefeated, we want to sign our names on our cabin wall," McLaren offered. Coach Grillo was not only a coach but also the founder and owner of the camp.

"We could add 'Cabin Aspen was sick all month!'" Cullen suggested.

"If we write that, people will think we were in here puking," Jagger Stephen said, pretending to gag.

The boys all laughed. "I guess I'll settle for 'Cabin Aspen, record breakers' then," Cullen said.

From his spot near the window Luke smiled along with the other campers, but his eyes were fixed on the lake outside. "I hope Blaine's walking Stanley every day," he said. "Otherwise that bulldog is going to turn into a bullhog!"

"My mom texted me. Blaine's skating backwards already!" Cullen said.

"That's awesome!" Lukey replied. "He'll be doing crossover drills soon. It'll be fun going to open skate with him this winter."

Cullen nodded. "We can make him 'it' for Pom-Pom-Pull Away."

"We have free time until tonight's dry land, guys," McLaren said. "Who's ready for another round of lake board hockey?"

The entire cabin jumped to their feet and put on their swim gear. Next, they went to Pinewood Lodge, the camp office, and grabbed water boards, plastic hockey sticks, and foam pucks. "Whoever created lake board hockey was a genius," Luke said.

When they reached the sandy beach around Clark Lake, Luke and Cullen fastened the floating nets to the water tanks. The boys jumped on their water boards. "Any game with a puck is a blast!" Cullen yelled, falling off his board after shooting the foam puck.

"Yup," Luke hollered. "Hockey in the rink, hockey on open water—life is good up north." He took a shot and sent waves crashing against the net.

"You got that right," Cullen said. "We got about two hours before dry land. Another game?"

CHAPTER

7

If You Think I'm Cute Now, Wait Until You See Me in My Team USA Jersey

"This pennant is perfect for Blaine's bedroom," Paisley said as she and Avery were shopping in the tournament souvenir store.

"How much?" asked Avery.

"Fifteen euros," replied Paisley. "Not bad."

"Yeah, and Blaine will love it!" Avery smiled wistfully. "I miss him."

"Me too," said Paisley. "But I'm excited to play in the championship game today. I love our Team USA jerseys!"

"It's such an honor to wear them," Avery said.

"Would you ever want to play in the Olympics, like Coach Lamoureux?" asked Paisley.

"Of course!" Avery said. "What's life without goals?" The girls high-fived each other.

Just then Coach Lamoureux came up. "But for now, playing here in Finland and bringing home the championship hardware is pretty cool, right?"

"*Sisu*, Coach!" Avery replied.

"Girls, you've got the grit, determination, and talent to go far," Coach Lamoureux said. "You should plan to play in college and after you graduate from college—for Team USA."

"College goals are set. UND and U of M, of course! Thanks, Coach. Looks like we're adding the Olympics to our bucket list!" Paisley said.

Coach's face grew serious. "And don't let anyone take goals off your bucket list. Doubt kills more dreams than failure ever will."

Paisley giggled. "Getting deep, Coach."

"I just believe in you. I've lived by working for a cause, not for applause. Now let's get going. We don't want to be late for the game," Coach Lamoureux said, hustling the girls away from the souvenir shop.

"Okay," Avery said. "I guess that championship trophy will be our souvenir."

The rosters for both teams were introduced for the championship game. The US players lined up on their blue line, holding pairs of sunglasses. The Canadian players, each holding a stick of ChapStick, lined up on their blue line.

The players removed their helmets and skated to center ice to exchange the hospitality gifts. Both national anthems played one after the other, then the puck was dropped.

Coach Lamoureux paced on the bench. She remembered her last Olympic game for the championship. It was the same matchup, Team USA versus Team Canada. "USA, you got this! Play tough right out of the gate!" she hollered, clapping her hands.

The first period didn't go as Team USA had hoped. The Canadians scored five fast goals, and at the end of the period Team USA was scoreless. Afterward, the players trudged into the locker room, defeated.

Coach Lamoureux soon joined her players. She was just as frustrated with their performance as they were. "You've got to think it, be it!" she said, looking each player in the eye. Avery and Paisley glanced at each other. They both knew what her words meant—she believed in them.

Avery stood. "We didn't come all the way to Finland just to eat pasties, tarts and *laxlada*! We came here to win for Team USA!"

Paisley rose to her feet. "We got this, girls!" she yelled. "Like Coach said, think it, be it!"

Their teammates let out shouts and whistles as they marched out of the locker room for period two. The second

period was opposite of the first. Team USA scored four fast, unanswered goals. Team Canada struggled to put the puck in the net. The period ended with the score 5-4.

The Team USA teammates cheered in their locker room while Coach Lamoureux listened from outside. She didn't go in. Instead she waited outside for the players to return to the ice. "Think it, be it!" she repeated as each player passed. Avery and Paisley both fist bumped their coach.

dear
hockey diary,

CHAPTER

8

The Hockey Diaries

Dear Hockey Diary,
   The summer flew by at Minnesota hockey camps! We had an absolute blast making new friends, making memories for a life time while dangling with fast hands and puck skills...
   Everyday, we "giver" with drills and conditioning dry land.

dry land   me   hills   "c" cullen
more hills   Aaron

holy moly did our speed increase! We loved lake board hockey!

sick! rad!

treats from the camp canteen rocked!

i-scream   best monster cookies   and

dogs   pizza   yeah, "c" has practiced his autograph...

Cabin Aspen went undefedted.
We were sick all month. Ha
Coach Grillo let us
leave our mark
inside Cabin Aspen
4 crushing
go jump in a lake the tourney
record.

Cabin Aspen
2016
Record Breakers!

But
Cabin Birch and Cabin Poplar
made it an epic battle.

We can't wait to get
home to see Blaine skate,
hang out with Stanley cup...
Oooh... and lead
Hockeytown USA back-to-state!
Go Hockeytown
USA!   Lukey
                                    Cullen

p.s. it will be o.k. 2c Aves and Fais 2

Dear Hockey Diary —

We are on the plane headed home! We carefully packed our second place medals.

Coach Lamouroux says you learn more in life sometimes, from losing. We lost by 1 goal.

This was a trip of a lifetime! We loved playing internationally and making new friends. We added to our bucket list...
Play in the Olympics!!
Go USA!!

KEEP CALM AND PLAY HOCKEY

a day without hockey is like a day without sunshine

"You miss 100% of the shots you don't take" — Wayne Gretzky

REAL GIRLS LOVE HOCKEY!!

DON'T GO THROUGH LIFE WITHOUT GOALS

Where friends turn into family

Guess you could say, this summer we went outside our comfort zone.

That's where the magic happens.

We can't wait to give Blaine his pennant, skate faster than Lukey and Cubben, and hug our families!

Oh, and lead Hockeytown USA back-to-state!

Sita mielta, On se!
♡ Pais and Aves ♡

P.S. I'm teaching myself calligraphy ~ cool!

"Every day is a great day for hockey." ~Mario Lemieux

HOCKEY is life

HOCKEY Girls Rule

NOT EVERY VICTORY SHOWS UP ON THE SCORE BOARD!

CHAPTER 9

Hockeytown USA ♥ Minnesota Bears

"Greattt Blainnne! Greatt Blainnne!" exclaimed Ann as Blaine walked into the decorated mezzanine area carrying his skates, helmet, and stick.

"Why hello, Ann," Blaine's mom said.

"Hi!" a peppy Ann replied.

"This will be a fun Sunday for the Minnesota Bears," Blaine's dad said.

"I-I-I-knnoow, and important!" Ann added, peeking at a table of silent auction items.

This Sunday was indeed extraordinary. The Minnesota Bears were hosting their annual end-of-summer hockey celebration and fundraiser. They were scheduled to play the children of current and former Minnesota Wild players with Ref Rylee and Ref Rosee officiating. After the game, the families, friends, and fans of the teams would celebrate with a BBQ and open skate.

This would be Blaine's first game since joining the Bears. He could barely contain his excitement as he looked at the walls of the arena, which were plastered with balloons and hand-painted signs.

"Anything good in the silent auction, Ann?" asked Blaine's dad.

"Yesss!" Ann said.

"Dadddd, cannn weee loookkk?" Blaine asked.

"You betcha, Blaine!" his mom said. "We love supporting ASHA and the Minnesota Bears. The money raised gives kids like you and Ann a chance to play hockey!"

"It's important," Ann chimed in.

"Yeesssss, itt issss!" Blaine added, giving his parents a thumbs-up.

Cullen, Lukey, and Avery walked into the arena. "Wow, Hockeytown USA celebrating in style again!" Avery remarked.

Paisley skated by the trio and tapped her stick against the glass. Her dad was on the bench, coaching the Wild kids' team. "Go, Paisley, go!" Lukey said.

The friends scanned the rink, looking for Blaine. "That's him! I see him!" Avery shouted.

"Go Blaine!" Luke hollered, banging his hands against the rink boards. He and Avery joined the other fans, parents, and families on the bleachers while Cullen remained close to the boards. He didn't want to be far from his little brother.

The game began, and the players began dashing across the ice. Cullen shouted "Go Blaine!" every time his brother took the ice. Then it happened. With Cullen watching every play from the rink corner, he yelled, "Shoot, Blaine, shoot!"

Blaine heard his brother. He took a hard rockin' shot. Swish! The puck landed in the net, right behind the goalie! Blaine's teammates rushed over to hug him and pat him on the head, nearly pushing him over.

Paisley skated over and asked Ref Rosee for the puck, then tossed it at Blaine.

"Champ, you rock! Here's your first goal puck!"

Blaine looked to the rink corner. Cullen was still clapping, as were his parents and friends in the bleachers.

Later on during the open skate, Ann directed a game of Pom-Pom-Pull Away. Every kid and Wild player loved it!

Afterward, everyone gathered their skates and belongings while they chatted. "My dad bid and won two weeks at Minnesota Hockey Camps!" Lukey said, overjoyed.

"We were a high bid too!" Cullen replied. "We get to lead the crowd in 'Let's Play Hockey' during puck drop at a Wild game."

"Oh, wwwooooowww!" Blaine whooped.

Ann laughed. "Yoouuuu beettterr prraccticcee, Greattt Blainnne," she said.

"Leeetttt'sss pllllaayyyy hoooccckkeyy! Letttssss playyy hoocckey! Letts pllayyy hockey! Lettssss ppplay hockey!" Blaine cheered.

Yes, let's play hockey!

ASK THE OFFICIALS
Rylee and Rosee's
Referee Resources

Important Words to Learn

ASHA: American Special Hockey Association, gives skaters of all abilities and talents the opportunity to play ice hockey.

canteen: A store that sells merchandise, food and drink at a camp.

dangle: An action of performing a move or deke with the puck.

diary: A book in which one keeps a daily record of events and experiences.

euro: The single European currency (money).

Finnish: The language spoken in Finland and in parts of Russia and Sweden.

grit: Courage and resolve; strength of character.

guffaw: A loud and boisterous laugh.

laxlada: Finnish salmon casserole.

mezzanine: A low story between two others in a building, typically between the ground and first floors.

Pom-Pom-Pull Away: A game, similar to tag, played on ice.

U of M: A college, named the University of Minnesota, is located in Minneapolis, MN.

UND: A college, named the University of North Dakota, is located in Grand Forks, ND.

MEET JAYNE AND KATRINA

Jayne wears many helmets, including college professor, lawyer, author, wife, mother, and serves as the national legal director for the American Special Hockey Association.

Katrina shares her high energy and love for all things creative as an artist, designer, decorator, illustrator, art educator, event planner, wife, mother, and even a hardware store owner.

Katrina shares her high energy and love for all things creative as an artist, designer, decorator, illustrator, art educator, event planner, wife, mother, and hardware store owner. Katrina is passionate about helping first-generation college students succeed, serving as an avid blood donor, and relaxing with DIY projects. Her true dream job will come, someday, as a grandma, proudly stocking "Grandma Katrina's library!"

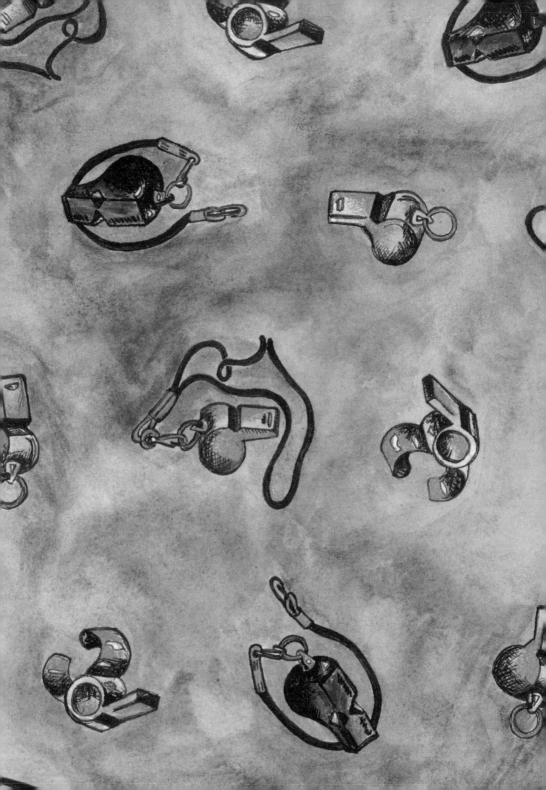